W9-BFU-451

LIBRARY
UNIVERSITY OF KENTUCKY

EDUCATION LIBRARY
UNIVERSITY OF KENTUCKY

RE-ZOOM

ISTVAN BANYAI

PUFFIN BOOKS

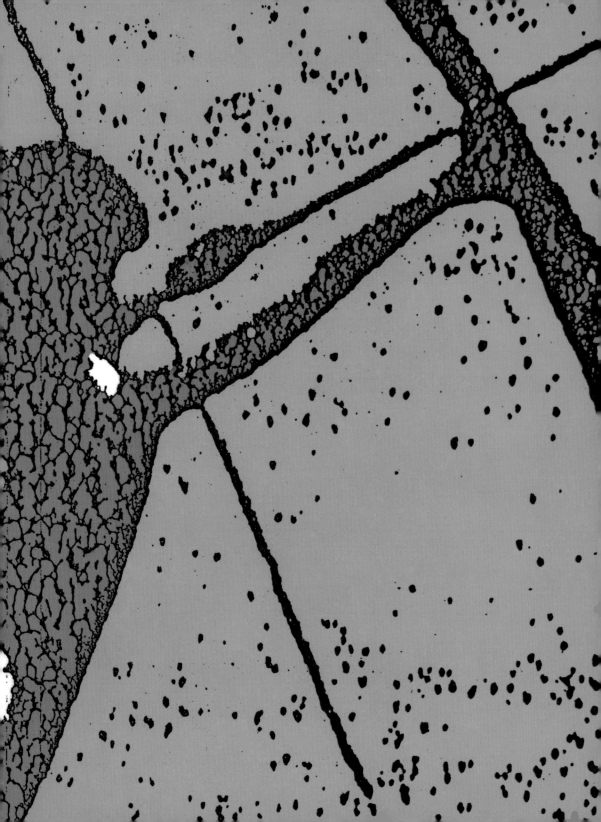

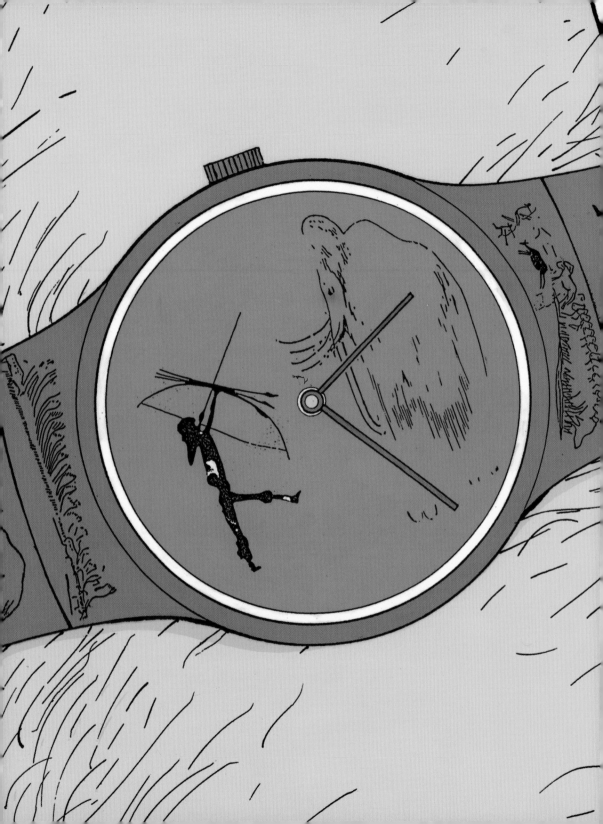

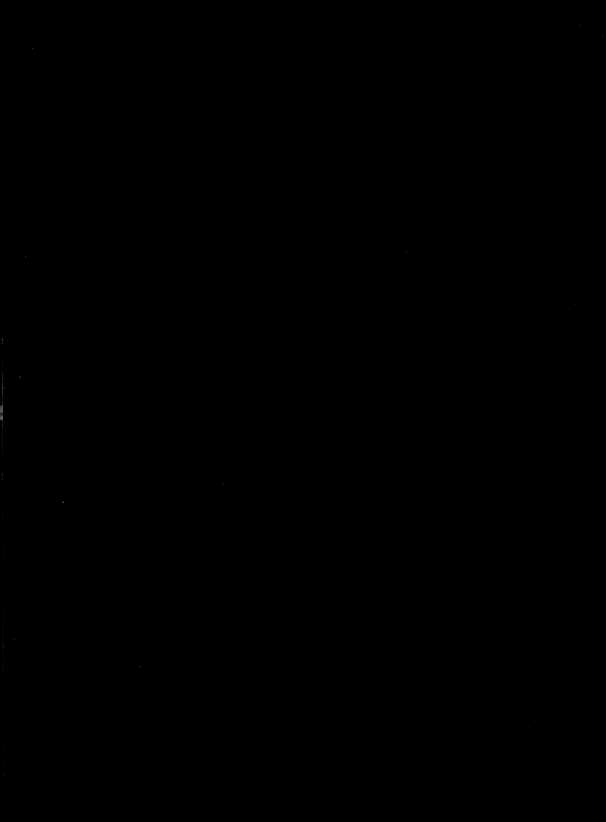

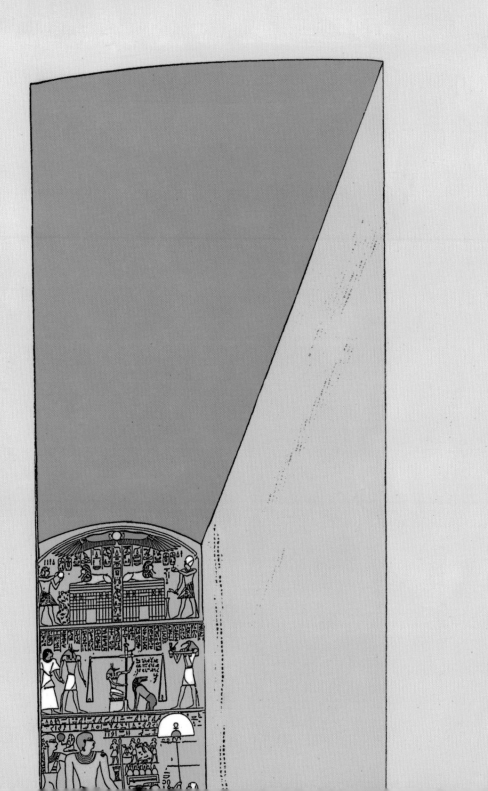

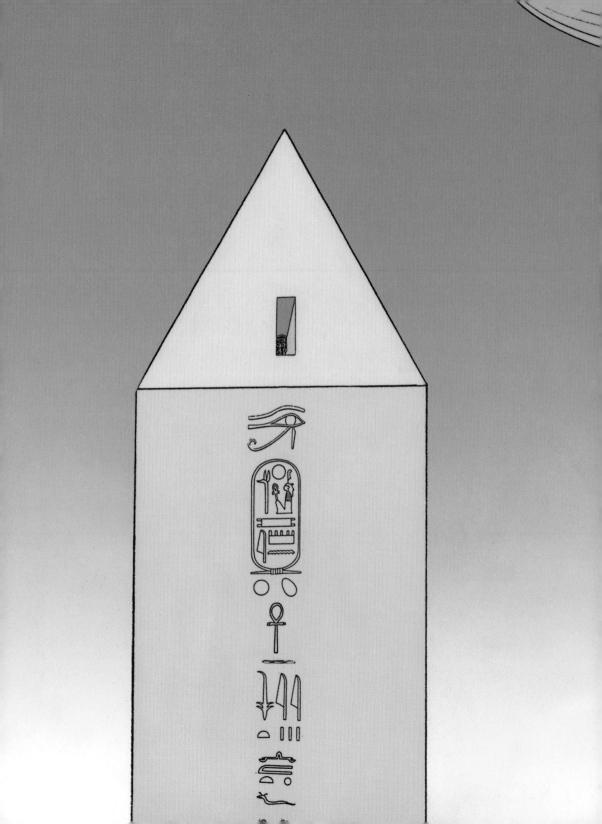

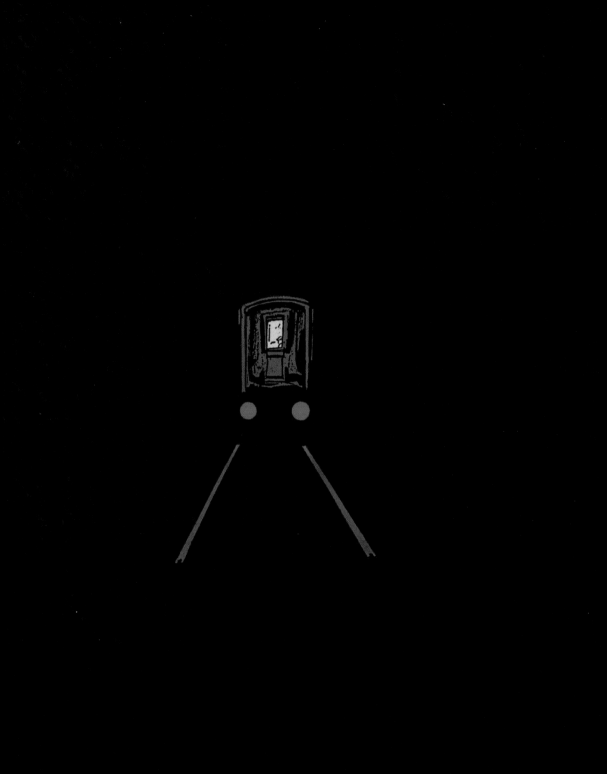

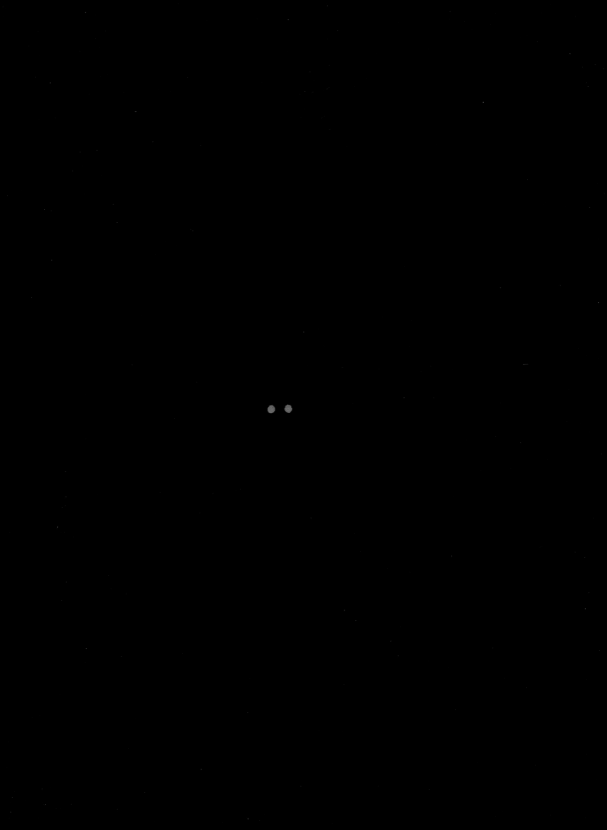

WITH SPECIAL THANKS TO
REGINA, BECKY, DAPHNE, MARGARET & NINA

PUFFIN BOOKS
PUBLISHED BY THE PENGUIN GROUP
PENGUIN PUTNAM INC., 345 HUDSON STREET, NEW YORK, NEW YORK 10014, U.S.A.
PENGUIN BOOKS LTD, 27 WRIGHTS LANE, LONDON W8 5TZ, ENGLAND
PENGUIN BOOKS AUSTRALIA LTD, RINGWOOD, VICTORIA, AUSTRALIA
PENGUIN BOOKS CANADA LTD, 10 ALCORN AVENUE, TORONTO, ONTARIO, CANADA M4V 3B2
PENGUIN BOOKS (N.Z.) LTD, 182-190 WAIRAU ROAD, AUCKLAND 10, NEW ZEALAND

PENGUIN BOOKS LTD, REGISTERED OFFICES: HARMONDSWORTH, MIDDLESEX, ENGLAND

FIRST PUBLISHED IN THE UNITED STATES OF AMERICA BY VIKING,
A DIVISION OF PENGUIN BOOKS USA INC., 1995
PUBLISHED BY PUFFIN BOOKS, A MEMBER OF PENGUIN PUTNAM BOOKS FOR YOUNG READERS, 1998

22 23 24 25 26 27 28 29 30

COPYRIGHT © ISTVAN BANYAI, 1995
ALL RIGHTS RESERVED

THE LIBRARY OF CONGRESS HAS CATALOGED THE VIKING EDITION AS FOLLOWS:
BANYAI, ISTVAN.
RE-ZOOM / BY ISTVAN BANYAI.   P.   CM.
SUMMARY: A WORDLESS PICTURE BOOK PRESENTS A SERIES OF SCENES, EACH ONE FROM FARTHER
AWAY, SHOWING, FOR EXAMPLE, A BOAT WHICH BECOMES THE IMAGE ON A
MAGAZINE, WHICH IS HELD IN A HAND, WHICH BELONGS TO A BOY, AND SO ON.
ISBN 0-670-86392-0
[1. VISUAL PERCEPTION—FICTION. 2. STORIES WITHOUT WORDS.] I. TITLE.
PZ7.B22947RE 1995 [E]—DC20 95-14265 CIP AC

PUFFIN BOOKS ISBN 978-0-14-055694-0

MANUFACTURED IN CHINA

FELIX THE CAT IMAGE USED BY PERMISSION OF DON ORIOLO
AND FELIX THE CAT PRODUCTIONS, INC. FELIX THE CAT IS
A REGISTERED TRADEMARK OF FELIX THE CAT PRODUCTIONS, INC.
© 1995 F.T.C.P., INC.

EXCEPT IN THE UNITED STATES OF AMERICA, THIS BOOK IS SOLD SUBJECT TO
THE CONDITION THAT IT SHALL NOT, BY WAY OF TRADE OR OTHERWISE, BE LENT,
RE-SOLD, HIRED OUT, OR OTHERWISE CIRCULATED WITHOUT THE PUBLISHER'S
PRIOR CONSENT IN ANY FORM OF BINDING OR COVER OTHER THAN THAT
IN WHICH IT IS PUBLISHED AND WITHOUT A SIMILAR CONDITION INCLUDING
THIS CONDITION BEING IMPOSED ON THE SUBSEQUENT PURCHASER.